Old MacDonald Had a Farm

Illustrated by
Kathi Ember

🌼 **A GOLDEN BOOK • NEW YORK**

Copyright © 1997 by Kathi Ember. All rights reserved. Published in the United States by Golden Books, an imprint of Random House Children's Books, a division of Random House, Inc., New York. GOLDEN BOOKS, A GOLDEN BOOK, A LITTLE GOLDEN BOOK, the G colophon, and the distinctive gold spine are registered trademarks of Random House, Inc.
www.goldenbooks.com
www.randomhouse.com/kids
Educators and librarians, for a variety of teaching tools, visit us at www.randomhouse.com/teachers
Library of Congress Control Number: 94-073369
ISBN: 978-0-307-98806-5
Printed in the United States of America
22 21 20 19 18 17 16

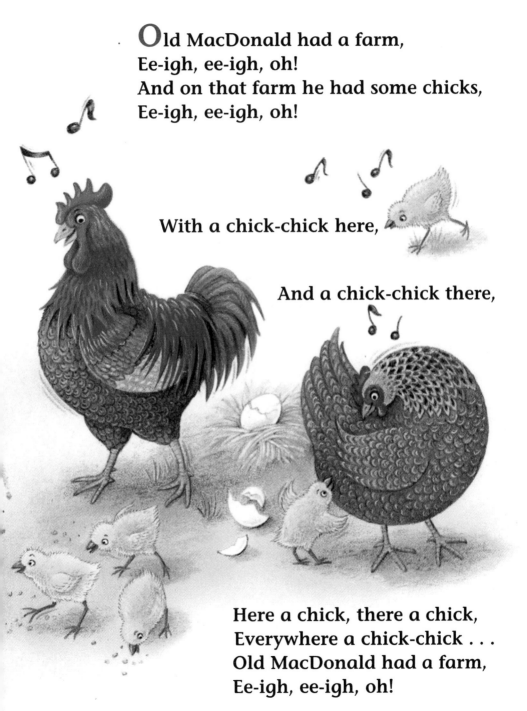

Old MacDonald had a farm,
Ee-igh, ee-igh, oh!
And on that farm he had some chicks,
Ee-igh, ee-igh, oh!

With a chick-chick here,

And a chick-chick there,

Here a chick, there a chick,
Everywhere a chick-chick . . .
Old MacDonald had a farm,
Ee-igh, ee-igh, oh!

And on that farm he had some horses,
Ee-igh, ee-igh, oh!

With a neigh-neigh here,

And a neigh-neigh there,

Here a neigh, there a neigh,
Everywhere a neigh-neigh . . .
Old MacDonald had a farm,
Ee-igh, ee-igh, oh!

And on that farm he had some turkeys,
Ee-igh, ee-igh, oh!

With a gobble-gobble here,

And a gobble-gobble there,

Here a gobble, there a gobble,
Everywhere a gobble-gobble . . .
Old MacDonald had a farm,
Ee-igh, ee-igh, oh!

And on that farm he had some pigs,
Ee-igh, ee-igh, oh!

With an oink-oink here,
And an oink-oink there,

Here an oink,
  there an oink,

Everywhere an oink-oink . . .

Old MacDonald had a farm,
Ee-igh, ee-igh, oh!

And on that farm he had some cows,
Ee-igh, ee-igh, oh!
With a moo-moo here,
And a moo-moo there,

Here a moo, there a moo,
Everywhere a moo-moo . . .
Old MacDonald had a farm,
Ee-igh, ee-igh, oh!

And on that farm he had some donkeys,
Ee-igh, ee-igh, oh!

With a hee-haw here,
And a hee-haw there,

Here a hee, there a haw,
Everywhere a hee-haw . . .
Old MacDonald had a farm,
Ee-igh, ee-igh, oh!

And on that farm he had some sheep,
Ee-igh, ee-igh, oh!

With a baa-baa here,
And a baa-baa there,

Here a baa, there a baa,
Everywhere a baa-baa.

With a hee-haw here,
And a hee-haw there,
Here a hee, there a haw,
Everywhere a hee-haw.

With a moo-moo here,
And a moo-moo there,
Here a moo, there a moo,
Everywhere a moo-moo.

With an oink-oink here,
And an oink-oink there,
Here an oink, there an oink,
Everywhere an oink-oink.

With a gobble-gobble here,
And a gobble-gobble there,
Here a gobble, there a gobble,
Everywhere a gobble-gobble.

With a neigh-neigh here,
And a neigh-neigh there,
Here a neigh, there a neigh,
Everywhere a neigh-neigh.

With a chick-chick here,
And a chick-chick there,
Here a chick, there a chick,
Everywhere a chick-chick.

Old MacDonald had a farm,
Ee-igh, ee-igh, oh!

Old MacDonald Had a Farm

Old Mac-Don-ald had a farm, Ee-igh, ee-igh,

oh! And on that farm he had some chicks,

Ee-igh, ee-igh, oh! With a chick-chick here, and a

chick-chick there, Here a chick, there a chick, Every-where a chick-chick.

Old Mac-Don-ald had a farm, Ee-igh, ee-igh, oh!